بسم الله الرحمن الرحيم

The Brave Boy

M. S. Kayani and Khurram Murad

The Islamic Foundation

ISBN 0 86037 112 3

MUSLIM CHILDREN'S LIBRARY

General Editors:
Khurram Murad and **Ahmad von Denffer**

THE BRAVE BOY

Authors:
M.S. Kayani and **Khurram Murad**

Illustrations:
Shamin Shahin

These stories are about the Prophet and his Companions and, though woven around authentic ahadith, should be regarded only as stories.

Published by:
The Islamic Foundation,
Markfield Dawah Centre,
Ratby Lane, Markfield,
Leicester LE67 9RN,
United Kingdom

Quran House,
PO Box 30611,
Nairobi, Kenya

PMB 3193,
Kano, Nigeria

British Library Cataloguing in Publication Data
Kayani, M.S.
   The brave boy. – (Muslim children's library; 10)
   I. Title   II. Murad, K.   III. Series
   823'.914(J) PZ7

ISBN 0-86037-112-3

Printed by Ashford Colour Press Ltd, Gosport, Hants.

MUSLIM CHILDREN'S LIBRARY

An Introduction

Here is a new series of books, but with a difference, for children of all ages. Published by the Islamic Foundation, the Muslim Children's Library has been produced to provide young people with something they cannot perhaps find anywhere else.

Most of today's children's books aim only to entertain and inform or to teach some necessary skills, but not to develop the inner and moral resources. Entertainment and skills by themselves impart nothing of value to life unless a child is also helped to discover deeper meaning in himself and the world around him. Yet there is no place in them for God, who alone gives meaning to life and the universe, nor for the divine guidance brought by His prophets, following which can alone ensure an integrated development of the total personality.

Such books, in fact, rob young people of access to true knowledge. They give them no unchanging standards of right and wrong, nor any incentives to live by what is right and refrain from what is wrong. The result is that all too often the young enter adult life in a state of social alienation and bewilderment, unable to cope with the seemingly unlimited choices of the world around them. The situation is especially devastating for the Muslim child as he may grow up cut off from his culture and values.

The Muslim Children's Library aspires to remedy this deficiency by showing children the deeper meaning of life and the world around them; by pointing them along paths leading to an integrated development of all aspects of their personality; by helping to give them the capacity to cope with the complexities of their world, both personal and social; by opening vistas into a world extending far beyond this life; and, to a Muslim child especially, by providing a fresh and strong faith, a dynamic commitment, an indelible sense of identity, a throbbing yearning and an urge to struggle, all rooted in Islam.

The books aim to help a child anchor his development on the rock of divine guidance, and to understand himself and relate to himself and others in just and meaningful ways. They relate directly to his soul and intellect, to his emotions and imagination, to his motives and desires, to his anxieties and hopes — indeed, to every aspect of his fragile, but potentially rich personality. At the same time it is recognised that for a book to hold a child's attention, he must enjoy reading it; it should therefore arouse his curiosity and entertain him as well. The style, the language, the illustrations and the production of the books are all geared to this goal. They provide moral education, but not through sermons or ethical abstractions.

Although these books are based entirely on Islamic teachings and the vast Muslim heritage, they should be of equal interest and value to all children, whatever their country or creed; for Islam is a universal religion, the natural path.

Adults, too, may find much of use in them. In particular, Muslim parents and teachers will find that they provide what they have for so long been so badly needing. The books will include texts on the Quran, the Sunnah and other basic sources and teachings of Islam, as well as history, stories and anecdotes for supplementary reading. Each book will cater for a particular age group, classified into: pre-school, 5-8 years, 8-11, 11-14 and 14-17.

We invite parents and teachers to use these books in homes and classrooms, at breakfast tables and bedside and encourage children to derive maximum benefit from them. At the same time their greatly valued observations and suggestions are highly welcome.

To the young reader we say: you hold in your hands books which may be entirely different from those you have been reading till now, but we sincerely hope you will enjoy them; try, through these books, to understand yourself, your life, your experiences and the universe around you. They will open before your eyes new paths and models in life that you will be curious to explore and find exciting and rewarding to follow. May God be with you forever.

And may He bless with His mercy and acceptance our humble contribution to the urgent and gigantic task of producing books for a new generation of people, a task which we have undertaken in all humility and hope.

Khurram Murad
Director General

4

contents

1
Ali and the Prophet Muhammad

The Prophet Muhammad (Peace and Blessings be upon him)* had an uncle called Abu Talib. Abu Talib had been very kind to Muhammad. It was he who had looked after the Blessed Prophet in his own house since Muhammad was six years old. All the time that Muhammad lived with Abu Talib, his uncle treated him like a son. He had given him all the love and care that a good father should. Muhammad in return had loved and honoured his uncle. The Blessed Prophet lived with Abu Talib until he got married to Khadija and then he moved to a house of his own.

When Abu Talib had a new son, Muhammad was delighted. He was as pleased as if he had had a son of his own. As soon as he heard that the baby had been born, he hurried to his uncle's house to see the boy.

The baby was in his mother's lap. He was small, clear-eyed and very handsome. The Blessed Prophet went to the little boy and kissed him on the forehead.

'What are you going to call him?' he asked.

'Ali', Abu Talib replied.

* Muslims are required to invoke Allah's blessing and peace upon the Prophet whenever his name is mentioned.

As time went by Muhammad got to know and love Ali. He became so fond of him that one day he went to Abu Talib and said, 'Uncle, I know you love me as a son. I want to ask you to do something for me. Give Ali to me and let him come and live in my house. Khadija, too, will be very happy. We shall look after him and care for him, as you did for me.'

Abu Talib loved the Blessed Prophet so much that he could not refuse his request. So Ali left his father's home and went to live with the Blessed Prophet. In time, Ali came to help the Blessed Prophet in his great work.

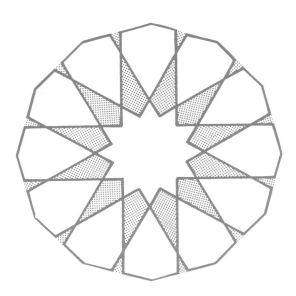

2
Ali becomes a Muslim

One day, when Ali was ten years old, he came home and saw something strange. Muhammad was standing with his head bent forward and his hands folded on his chest. His wife, Khadija, was also standing beside him, doing the same thing.

As Ali watched them, Muhammad and Khadija bowed towards the ground. They stayed in that position for a moment and then stood up straight again. Ali wondered what they were doing. Then he saw them go down on their knees and touch the ground with their foreheads. 'What a strange thing to do!,' thought Ali. 'I have often seen people bowing down before stone idols, but there is no idol here. Muhammad and Khadija are certainly not worshipping an idol, but they are worshipping Someone.'

Ali was a sensible boy. Although he did not completely understand what Muhammad was doing, he knew he was praying. He thought Muhammad was praying to a God whom he could not see. Ali very much wanted to know who this Unseen God was.

As soon as Muhammad had finished his Prayer, Ali asked him what he had been doing. Muhammad was pleased when the boy asked him to explain. He smiled at Ali and said to him, 'Listen carefully my boy! Khadija and I were worshipping Allah. He is

the One and only True God. There is no God but He.

'Allah has chosen me to be His Messenger. He has ordered me to take His message to my people. This is His message and this is what I have to tell the people. They should give up all false gods and worship only Him. They must obey Him alone, because He is the One and only True God.'

Muhammad then looked Ali straight in the eyes and said to him. 'You know how much I love you. I have looked after you as if you were my own son. I have never told you a lie — I have never deceived you. I want you to believe the truth that I have just told you. There is no God but Allah; He has chosen me as His Prophet.'

Ali knew at once that Muhammad was speaking the truth and so he believed what Muhammad had said. The Prophet (Peace and Blessings be upon him) was delighted. 'Welcome, Ali,' he said. 'You know in your heart what I have said is true. I can see you have accepted Allah as the One and only True God. You are the first boy to become a Muslim.'

3
Abu Talib
is worried about Ali

One day Ali was performing his Prayer with the Prophet (Peace and Blessings be upon him). They were praying with a few other Muslims in a secret mountain pass near Makka. Suddenly Ali's father, Abu Talib appeared. He had come to look for his son. Abu Talib was a kind old man who often worried about Ali. When he saw how Muhammad and Ali were praying, he wondered what they were doing. He had never seen anyone pray like that before and he began to feel uneasy.

When Abu Talib saw that they had finished praying, he went over to them.

'Muhammad' he said, 'What on earth are you doing?'

'We are praying,' the Blessed Prophet told him.

'How can you be praying?' he said. 'Where are the gods to which you should pray?'

'When we pray, we do not pray to gods of stone,' replied the Blessed Prophet.

'To whom then are you praying?'

'We pray to Allah the One and only True God.'

'But why do you pray to Him?'

'Because I am the Messenger of Allah. It is He who

has told me to pray to Him alone. Come uncle, join with us and worship Allah.'

When he heard this, Abu Talib replied, 'How can I? I am an old man. I cannot join you and give up the religion of my own tribe.'

'But don't you see?' said the Blessed Prophet. 'This is the true religion of our forefather Abraham'.

Abu Talib then went up to his son Ali, who was standing with the other Muslims.

'What are you doing here, my son,' he asked him. 'Have you also given up the religion of our forefathers?'

Ali, young though he was, said to his father, 'I have chosen to serve Allah. I am going to follow His Prophet Muhammad.'

When Abu Talib heard this he was worried. He was afraid that Ali was going to be led astray. He feared his son had given up the religion of his forefathers and this made him sad. He asked Ali to come back home and live with him. But Ali, although he loved his father dearly, did not want to go.

The Blessed Prophet saw how upset Abu Talib was and so turning to Ali he said, 'Ali, you are free to do as you like. If you would like to go back and live with your father, please do.'

Ali replied that he would rather stay with the Blessed Prophet and serve Allah.

So Abu Talib left his son Ali with the Blessed Prophet. He did not know what to do. He was unhappy because Ali had changed his religion. But he knew that Muhammad was a good and honest man. As he left, he said to the Blessed Prophet, 'Although I do not understand your religion, I trust you. You would never lead Ali into anything bad or evil. This I do know'.

4
Ali becomes a man

Ali was a good boy. He was kind and considerate. He also knew how to work hard. One day, when he was about eleven years old, the Prophet Muhammad (Peace and Blessings be upon him) called Ali to him . 'I want to give a feast to the elders of our family,' he said. 'I would like you to be in charge of all the preparations. You must also invite the guests.' Ali felt very honoured that the Blessed Prophet had asked him to be in charge of the feast. He invited all the elders of the family and saw to it that the food was properly prepared.

All the elders of the family came to the feast. Among them was Abu Lahab, who was one of the Blessed Prophet's uncles. Abu Lahab was an evil man. Throughout his life, all he had thought about was making money. He would do anything to make money. He used to tell lies. He used to cheat the poor. He even bullied those who could not fight back. The only thing that Abu Lahab loved was his wealth.

Like the other elders, Abu Lahab also worshipped idols made of stone. He refused to serve Allah as the One and only True God. He used to say to himself, 'If I became a Muslim, I would have to give some of my money to the poor and needy. This is what Allah says we should do. If I became a Muslim, I would have to be honest. I would not be

free to make money by telling lies and cheating'.

After the elders had eaten, Muhammad the Blessed Prophet rose to speak to them about Allah. Muhammad wanted to tell them that Allah was the only True God and that he was His Prophet. He also wanted to tell them to stop worshipping stone idols.

No sooner had the Blessed Prophet started to speak, than Abu Lahab began to shout him down. Abu Lahab hated the Blessed Prophet even though he was his nephew. He did not want the other guests to hear what Muhammad was going to say. He shouted so loudly that the Blessed Prophet had to stop speaking. So all the guests went away without hearing what the Blessed Prophet had to say about Allah.

When the guests had gone, Ali was very upset. He was disappointed with Abu Lahab. He could not understand how one of his own family could behave so badly. The Blessed Prophet saw how upset Ali was and said to him 'Do not give up hope, Ali. You will see. We shall win because Allah will help us. I want you to prepare another feast and invite the same guests. We shall see what happens this time.'

Ali did as the Blessed Prophet asked him to do. All the elders of the family came to the feast. After they had eaten, the Blessed Prophet again rose to speak to them about Allah. This time Abu Lahab did not interrupt.

'My friends,' the Blessed Prophet said. 'I am here with a message from your Lord. Allah, the One and only True God, has chosen me as His Prophet. He has sent me as His Messenger to tell you how to live your life to attain success in this world and in the Hereafter. Listen carefully to what Allah has told me to tell you. This is what He says:

I am the only True God.
Remember Me always.
Love Me and worship Me.
Serve Me and obey Me.
Bow down before Me.

If you do this, you will please Me.
And I shall make you a promise because I love and care for you. If you do exactly as I say, I shall reward you generously and deliver you from all evil. Have no fear, nor will you regret anything.

This is what Allah has said to me. This is what he told me to tell you. Now, my brothers, which of you will help me serve Allah? Who will be my follower? Who will be my companion in His great work?'

No one said a word. Although all the elders heard what the Blessed Prophet had said, no one came forward to help him. When the Blessed Prophet looked at each of them in turn, they turned their faces away from him. Ali could not believe it. He knew in his heart that Muhammad had spoken the truth but he could not understand why the elders did not believe him. 'They must be mad if they don't want Allah to guide them.'

Ali looked towards the Blessed Prophet who was standing waiting for someone to offer to help him. Ali could bear the stony silence no longer. Quietly he got to his feet. Then he went right through the middle of the elders and stood by the Blessed Prophet's side.

'Prophet of Allah,' he said, 'I shall be your follower. I shall be your companion and helper. Although I am young and not very strong, I shall fight by your side. Your enemies will be my enemies.'

When the elders heard what Ali had to say, they did not know what to do. How could a boy help Muhammad fight his enemies? But Ali had faith in Allah. He knew that Allah would help him and the Blessed Prophet. He knew that one day they would win.

The Blessed Prophet was delighted at what Ali had done. 'Look,' he said, 'here is a boy who has more courage than all the men gathered here. I gladly welcome him as my follower and helper. You should all listen to him and follow him.'

Muhammad smiled at Ali. This was more than Abu Lahab could stand. He had been sitting there, quietly laughing to himself. But when he heard the Blessed Prophet praising Ali, he began to shout again and make a terrible noise.

'Brothers,' he said. 'How can a man and a boy change the rest of the world? How can two persuade millions to follow them? It is not possible.'

But Abu Lahab was wrong. This is just what the Blessed Prophet and Ali and others who followed the Blessed Prophet did do, because Allah was with them.

5
The feat of courage

The Prophet Muhammad (Peace and Blessings be upon him) spent most of his life trying to get the people of Makka to worship Allah alone. Every day he would go out into the city and tell them that Allah was the One and only True God. He would tell them that he was Allah's Prophet. Some of the people believed what Muhammad said and became Muslims. They worshipped Allah and trusted His Prophet. But although Muhammad tried hard for many years, the people of Makka who became Muslims, were few in number.

Most of the people of Makka refused to believe the Blessed Prophet. They were blinded by their own greed. They worshipped idols made of stone and hoped that these idols would make them rich and happy. The priests and leaders of the people also encouraged them to do this. They too were blinded by greed. They thought it right to make as much money as they could. They did not care how the money was made. The priests and leaders of the people refused to worship Allah, as the One and only True God.

Although the Blessed Prophet Muhammad had only a few followers, they were strong in their faith. Some of the people began to take notice of them and talk about them. 'Perhaps there is something in what these Muslims are doing,' they thought. 'Muhammad may be right. Perhaps we should give up worshipping idols made of stone and believe in Allah.'

When the priests and leaders of the people heard this sort of talk, they became very angry.'We shall lose all our power and wealth if the people believe Muhammad,' they said. 'There is only one thing to do to stop this. We must kill him.'

So the priests and leaders of the people made a secret plot to kill Muhammad, the Blessed Prophet. They chose some strong young men, one from each noble family in Makka, and armed them with sharp swords. They ordered the young men to surround the Blessed Prophet's house during the night. They were told to kill Muhammad as he left the house next morning. 'But you must be careful,' they said to the young men. 'You must keep a close eye on Muhammad during the night to see that he does not get away. You must take it in turn to watch him as he sleeps. If you do that, you will know the exact time when he wakes. You can then be ready for him as he leaves the house.'

But because the Blessed Prophet Muhammad was Allah's Messenger, Allah protected him and saved his life. Allah told Muhammad in advance of his enemies' plan. He ordered the Blessed Prophet to leave Makka at once and go to Yathrib where other Muslims were eagerly waiting for him. These would look after and care for him.

After Allah had told the Blessed Prophet of the plot to kill him, Muhammad called Ali to him.

'Allah has just told me that the house is going to be surrounded by my enemies. They have swords and are going to wait until the morning, when they will kill me. Tonight, when I go to sleep, they will keep a close watch on my bed. If I leave now, I can get clear away from Makka. They will not be able to catch me. But if I leave my bed unslept in they will know I have left. Would you sleep in my bed tonight? If you cover yourself well, they will not be able to see your face. They will then think that I am sleeping there. In the morning they will discover the truth but by then I shall be on my way to Yathrib.'

Ali was very willing to help the Blessed Prophet and readily agreed to his plan. He dearly loved Muhammad and was only too happy to serve him in any way he could. So Muhammad left his house secretly, without his enemies knowing that he had gone.

When the Blessed Prophet had gone, Ali was left alone in the house. He crawled into the Blessed Prophet's bed and drew the covers over his head. As he went to sleep, he knew that the enemies of the Blessed Prophet had surrounded the house. But Ali was not afraid of them. He slept soundly all night. He knew that what he was doing was dangerous. When the Blessed Prophet's enemies found out the truth, they might kill him instead. This

did not trouble Ali because he loved and feared only Allah.

While Ali was asleep, the enemies of the Blessed Prophet kept watch outside. They imagined that it was Muhammad the Blessed Prophet who was sleeping in the bed. They waited impatiently for the dawn. Then they would seize the Blessed Prophet and kill him.

When the dawn came they entered the house and stood in amazement. To their horror it was not the Blessed Prophet who rose from the bed, but Ali, his young cousin. They could not believe this because they had kept such a close watch on the house. They became even more angry when they found that the Blessed Prophet was nowhere to be found in the house. They began to rant and rave. They rushed through the rooms searching everywhere for the Blessed Prophet. Finally they took hold of Ali and screamed at him:

'Where is Muhammad? Come on, tell us. He is hiding somewhere, isn't he?'

'Muhammad, the Prophet of Allah, the One and only True God, has left Makka,' Ali replied calmly. 'He is not here and you cannot find him now.'

'Come on then,' they shouted, 'tell us where he has gone. We can chase after him and catch him. If you do not tell us, we will beat you without mercy.'

Once again Ali replied calmly, 'Muhammad the Prophet has left Makka. That is all I am going to tell you.' And that is all Ali did tell them.

When they heard this, the enemies of the Blessed Prophet went away.

A few days later, with the help of Allah, the Blessed Prophet arrived safely at Yathrib, which later came to be called Madina al-nabi, the City of the Prophet.

Later, when Ali met Muhammad, the Blessed Prophet asked him, 'Were you not afraid when my enemies threatened to beat you?'

'No,' replied Ali. 'I fear none but Allah.'

6
An unequal fight

Five years had passed since the Prophet (Peace and Blessings be upon him) had come to Madina. The armies from Makka had attacked him twice and he had fought battles at Badr and Uhud. Now, once again the enemy armies had arrived. This time they had mobilised the Blessed Prophet's enemies from all over Arabia and had come in full strength to surround the Holy City of Madina. Some 24,000 men had come to destroy Islam and the tiny band of Muslims who lived in the Blessed Prophet's Holy City.

Yet, the servants of Allah did not fear them.

Even though they were few in number, in arms and horses, they were strong in their faith in Allah and His Blessed Prophet. So strong was this faith that they knew for certain that if they should die fighting in this cause, Allah would grant them Paradise.

As the armies of the Quraysh, the Banu Kinana and the people of Tihama approached, they beheld a sight which caused them dismay and astonishment. Before them lay an obstacle which they had never before encountered. A gaping trench, completely surrounding the city, had been dug by the Blessed Prophet and his followers in order to protect Madina from the onslaught of the enemy.

Feverishly, the Quraysh mounted their steeds and galloped towards the trench at full speed. But the horses, eyeing the deep chasm before them, skidded to a halt and refused to attempt the leap in spite of the shouts and lashes from their masters.

Wave after wave of cavalry attempted the leap, but each time they were forced to abandon the attempt. Finally there arrived the greatest horseman of all. Mighty 'Amr, clad in iron armour and dazzling helmet, sat like a giant upon his horse. His keen eye appraised the situation in an instant. Back and forth he rode with his men searching for a place where the trench was narrower. Before long he found such a place and his horse cleared the trench with a giant leap.

'Amr was now on the swampy ground between the trench and the mount of Sal'. Not far off, the Muslims watched anxiously. They were under siege and surrounded, but they were prepared to fight. Ali was commanding the forces which were guarding that point of the trench. He had seen 'Amr before at the battle of Badr and knew this warrior to be as tough as the iron armour he wore, and very brave and courageous.

'Amr wasted no time in delivering his challenge to single combat:

'Who dares fight me?' he roared.

A hush fell over the Believers as they recognised the voice. All eyes turned towards the Blessed Prophet. Ali stepped up with anticipation, but the Blessed

Prophet raised his hand. 'Don't you see, it is 'Amr!,' he warned.

Again the cry rang out: 'Come on, Muslims, are there no takers for Paradise today?' he sneered.

Ali clenched his teeth and grasped the hilt of his sword. Again he asked the Blessed Prophet's permission to meet this giant and silence him once and for all. But again the Blessed Prophet held him back.

In the Arab custom, 'Amr hurled his next challenge in verse:

> Here I stand, 'Amr the Proud
> Hoarse am I from shouting loud
> Muslim cowards, hear my call!
> I challenge the first to his downfall!'

The Blessed Prophet realising now that it was hopeless to try to hold back fearless Ali in the face of such taunting, gave him the sign to go ahead. Little Ali clutched his heavy sword and marched forward, chanting as he went:

> 'My mind is clear, my faith holds fast
> Truth shall conquer all at last
> O hasty 'Amr, your challenge I meet
> You shall, by Allah, die at my feet!'

The giant stared with amazement at the spindly little man before him. He began to roar with laughter. Then he shook his head in pity. 'O 'tis a shame. I would hardly bother to shed the blood of a

puny little man like you. Send one of your uncles who is older than you.'

But Ali stood his ground. 'I want to fight you, and by Allah I shall kill you,' he repeated.

The sheer impudence of such a statement threw 'Amr into a rage. He drew his sword and spurred his horse forward.

Ali said to him, 'How can I fight you on a horse?'

'Amr dismounted. He then lunged forward and brought his sword down with full force upon Ali. But Ali raised his shield, and with a crash, sword and shield locked together, the blade embedded deeply into the shield. 'Amr, crimson with anger, tugged at his sword with such force that it flew back and gashed his neck. As his huge bulk tottered, Ali smote the final blow. A cloud of dust rose, hiding the pair, and when it lifted, the Muslims cried out 'Allahu Akbar!' 'Amr had been slain. And through the grace of God Ali had killed him.

Ali, too young and too weak to be a soldier, had, because of his faith and courage, killed the mightiest of the enemy soldiers. Ali lifted his head, smiled at the Blessed Prophet, and recited for all to hear:

> 'This foolish man served gods of stone
> Only Allah serve I, for He is One
> O enemies of Allah, remember well
> Who fights the Prophet lands in Hell!'

7
He who loved Allah and His Messenger

Khaybar was a strong fortress located about 100 kilometres to the north of Madina. Held by Jewish tribes, Khaybar was in the forefront of the wars being waged by the Quraysh against the Muslims in Madina. When all the armies of Makka and all the tribes of Arabia allied with the Quraysh came to surround Madina in the battle of al-Ahzab, when the fight between Ali and 'Amr took place, the Jews of Khaybar were instrumental in uniting these tribes and inciting them to attack Madina. The Muslims knew that Madina would never be safe until Khaybar was subdued.

In the seventh year of Hijra, after the Prophet (Peace and Blessings be upon him) had arranged a treaty with the Makkans at Hudaibia, he now made his move towards Khaybar.

Khaybar consisted of a number of fortresses. The Blessed Prophet conquered one fort after another. The first to fall was the fort of Na'im; then al-Qamus. Next to be conquered was the fort of al-Sa'b and finally the two forts at al-Watih and al-Sulalim.

The siege took a long time because each fort was very strongly built and heavily reinforced. One of the forts which had been under siege for a long time proved very hard to overcome. It held firm against onslaught after onslaught. No one could conquer it. Finally the Blessed Prophet called his men about him and announced: 'Tomorrow I will give the flag to a man who loves Allah and His Messenger. Because Allah and His Prophet love him, by his hand will the fort be conquered.'

Everyone waited anxiously to see who that favoured man would be. Each one wished in his own heart he could be that man. When morning came, the Blessed Prophet called Ali to him. The Blessed Prophet handed him the white flag. 'Ali,' he said, 'take this flag and go forth until God grants you victory.'

Now at the time, Ali was suffering from an eye infection. He wondered how he would be able to undertake such a mission while being unable to see properly. The Blessed Prophet carefully tilted Ali's head and using his own saliva as a balm, rubbed it on Ali's eyes. To Ali's astonishment he was able to see clearly again. Ali then asked the Blessed Prophet: 'O Messenger of Allah, shall I fight them till they become Muslims?'

The Blessed Prophet said: 'When you reach the fort, first send your emissary to them, invite them to Islam and inform them that they must bear oath to worship none but Allah. By Allah, even if one man comes to the right path through your efforts the reward will be greater for you than a hundred swift-footed camels.'

Ali went forward with a small force. He reached the fort and stuck the flag in a pile of rocks near to the wall. 'Who are you,' called a Jew from the top of the fort.

Ali said: 'I am Ali, son of Abu Talib, cousin of Muhammad.'

Immediately the whole garrison streamed out of the fort to fight them. One of the soldiers advanced toward Ali and struck him in such a way that his shield fell from his hand. Ali appeared to be filled with such miraculous strength that he was able to grab a door of the fort and use it as a shield. Armed with this heavy door for protection he fought bravely until God gave him victory. When the fighting was over he let it fall to the ground.

Abu Rafi, who was with Ali on this expedition, says that later he and seven others tried to turn that door over but they were unable to move it. Such was the power invested in Ali by Allah the Merciful.

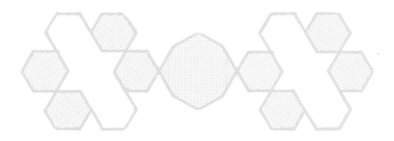